Miz Fannie Mae's Fine New Easter Hat

by Melissa Milich 🌼 Illustrated by Yong Chen

SCHOLASTIC INC.
New York Toronto London Auckland Sydney

To my parents, Nick and Elaine — M. M.

To Hong, Kai, and Ellen — Y. C.

Acknowledgments

I'd like to acknowledge Greg Voss for his love and support; my editor, Megan Tingley, and her assistant, Erica Stahler, at Little, Brown; all the Sydnors for making me feel like a member of their family; and Andrew Christie, a great writer, for his help with the ending.

ISBN 0-590-68414-0

12 11 10 9 8 7 6 5 4 3 2   8 9/9 0 1 2 3/0

Printed in the U.S.A.   14

First Scholastic printing, January 1998

$\mathcal{M}$ama always says the kind of hat you wear on your head is not so important as the thoughts inside it. But this year Daddy said, "You're absolutely right, Fannie Mae. And the thoughts inside *my* head keep telling me it's time you had a fine new Easter hat." So Daddy and I hatched a plan to make this special shopping trip ourselves. The morning before Easter, we were going to ride all the way into Meridian City to buy Mama a hat to wear to church.

Before we left, Mama took me aside. "I'm counting on you, Tandy. Ain't no way anyway I'm going to be letting him do something as important as buying a lady's Easter hat by himself."

"Yes, Mama," I said.

"Now, be sure not to let Daddy spend all his money."

"Yes, Mama."

"And don't let him be coming home with no ugly hat."

"No, Mama! I sure won't."

And then my little sister and brothers came out on the porch still in their pajamas to say good-bye. And the wind all those hands made waving at once blew us on a right good start to Meridian City.

From our wagon I could really see that spring had painted a pretty picture on the countryside. To me, this time of year has always been full of surprises, more so than Christmas. The bare trees from the winter suddenly get the first leaves on them like a lady putting on her gloves. Then before you know it, that same tree is giving you pieces of fruit so big they take two hands to hold, and the birds are making nests in the trees. Even though you see the same thing year after year, somehow each spring, it all looks brand new.

Our horse, Brown Sugar, clop-clippety-clopped all the way to Meridian City, twenty-five miles away. The big city made me nervous, but Daddy acted like we fit right in. Folks walked fast and dressed fancy, and the streets were crowded with automobiles.

Most people who go to our church back at home on the mountain would pick out a hat from the General Store, or if they were really serious about looking good, they ordered their hats through the Sears catalog, but I knew Daddy wanted to find a hat for Mama like no other. I tried not to think about how we could afford that. Mama was always talking about how poor we were, but whenever she started in, Daddy would practically pick Mama up with one arm and grab a couple of us kids with the other, and say, "Look how rich we are! I feel like I'm the richest man in the world."

We went directly to a place called The Millinery Shop, which Daddy said is a fancy way to say women's hats. "You have to be a *millionaire-y* to shop here," he said, chuckling.

The hats in that store came in all shapes, sizes, colors, and fashionable taste — tall hats and cone hats, square hats and beanie hats. Daddy and I started at one end of the store and worked our way around. I saw all manner of geographic wonderment: hats that looked like volcanoes erupting and fruit gardens to rival Eden. My daddy was a very careful shopper and tried on a lot of hats. I tried them on, too. Daddy even tried on the ugly ones!

"That's just so to know what I don't like," he said.

There was a moment when I thought he was going to buy this hat that would have sat clumsy as a washing machine on top of Mama's head. There was even a tag on the ugly hat that said "Price Reduced," and I held my breath while Daddy tried it on.

But he knew it was not good enough for Mama. Then I happened to look up and see a hat sitting all by itself up on top of a glass display case. The store owner brought over a ladder to bring it down. The hat was draped with lace and netting and had both fruit and flowers growing on it like a fancy garden. And nestled in a bed of leaves were four little speckled eggs. My daddy had hands like bread baked too long, but he handled that hat as if the delicate eggs on it might actually break.

"How much is it?" I asked.

The store owner raised his eyebrows but didn't say a word. There was a tag on a string attached to the hat, and he just turned it over to let us have a look at the price.

Daddy puckered his lips to a low whistle. "Is this the one, Tandy?"

I nodded.

"Well then, I always say nothing is too good for your Mama."

"A very good choice indeed," said the store owner, and Daddy shook hands with him, then the store owner shook hands with me, and then I shook hands with Daddy. The store owner wrapped up the hat, and Daddy and I started the long ride home, Mama's new hat on the seat beside us, the prettiest hat in all of Meridian City. We couldn't wait to show it to Mama, and I begged Brown Sugar to please try going just a bit faster. *Clippety-clop-clop-clop.*

We saw the look on Mama's face as soon as we got home. But it wasn't the happy look we had been expecting. She had been working in the kitchen, making cakes for Easter, and so she washed up while we stood there with the new hat, but she dried off her hands slowly before she came over to see.

"Don't you like it?" I asked.

I think she *did* like it. In fact, I think she fell in love with it the moment she saw it, but she said, "A hat that beautiful cost way too much money for things we're needing worse. You need to take it back to the store and get your money back, Hayman."

And then she went back to her baking and didn't look at the hat anymore, almost as if she didn't want to get attached to something she knew she shouldn't keep. I was waiting for Daddy to make it all better. I was waiting for him to grab us all and say how rich we were. But he didn't do that. He didn't get mad or look hurt—none of that. All he said was "Whatever you want, Fannie Mae." He took the hat and hung it next to his milk-delivering cap on the rack near the front door. Then he went into the living room and sat at his big chair near the radio. Daddy winked at me and said, "Don't you worry, Tandy."

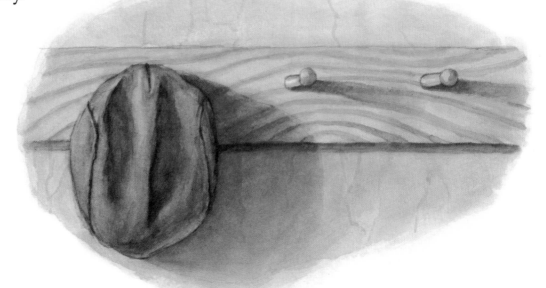

The next morning Daddy got up so early, he put the Easter Bunny to shame. He had to deliver the milk on Easter just like any other day, but when I passed by the hat rack, I noticed the cap he always wore was still hanging there. "Where's Daddy?" I asked.

"You know he's doing the milk route, Tandy."

"But he left his cap."

"It's not like him to forget that," Mama said, and at that moment she and I both noticed that there was indeed one certain hat missing from the rack.

Yes, Daddy delivered all his milk that Easter morning wearing Mama's fine new hat the entire time. Those cold creamy milk bottles tinkled against each other like a lot of cheery music. By then the rest of the folks in our parts were just starting to wake up and they called out to him, "Fine hat, Hayman!"

My daddy waved back. "None finer!"

When the last bottle was delivered, Daddy pulled up to our house in his wagon. He was still wearing the hat, and Mama came out to meet him.

"Well, I can't take this hat back to the store now, Fannie Mae," Daddy said. "It's already been worn. I guess you're going to have to keep it."

Mama put her hands on her hips and said, "I'm not going to wear that hat to church, Hayman. Everybody's seen it already!"

But I could see Mama was just tickled, and she let Daddy put that hat right directly on her own head, where it belonged.

Then Daddy grouped us all together like we were waiting on somebody to take a picture, even though we didn't own a camera. But Daddy said he was taking a picture of us in his memory that he would keep with him forever. Daddy was so proud of us all looking so good that day, but he was most proud of Mama, and she looked right beautiful in that hat of hers.

We were practically a parade walking down the road. Daddy was humming an old song about an Easter bonnet and sure in a good mood. And everybody we saw along the way admired Mama's hat.

"Those eggs look real, Sister Fannie Mae," said Miss Sophia Rathbone.

"Yes, they do, don't they?" and Mama touched the edges of her hat proudly.

"Ate one this morning matter of fact," my daddy joked.

Most of the other ladies at Solid Rock wore new hats, too, and it seemed that the ladies who wore the biggest hats always sat in the row right directly in front of our family, their heads tilted back with all the weight. That Easter was one of unusually big hats. Mrs. Georgia Rae Brooks sported a flying saucer ready for takeoff, and Sister Sophia Rathbone's resembled a five-pound can of coffee atop of her head. Mrs. Margaret M. Otis wore a hat the size of the state of Texas, with the Lone Star on it. I couldn't hardly see the choir what with all the hats blocking my view!

Preacher Jurkins got hot with his sermon right away. He was retelling the Easter story like we had never heard it before, and his words and the humming of the choir in the background stirred us so that we were prime for a miracle.

"THERE WAS A GARDEN WHERE NO ONE HAD EVER BEEN LAID . . ."

The ushers had left the church doors open because it was a truly hot day. The ladies were batting their fans most fervently, and the preacher's voice started boiling, and a bird even flew in from outside and settled on the rafters above our heads like it belonged in church, too!

"FOR AN ANGEL OF THE LORD DESCENDED FROM HEAVEN AND SAT UPON IT . . ."

And just when Preacher Jurkins was sweating the hardest, and the ladies' fans flapped back and forth the most furious, something surprising happened.

One, then two, of those eggs on Mama's hat started to crack.

"AND THE ANGEL SAID, BE NOT AFRAID!"

I was staring at the back of Mama's head, at her fine new Easter hat with the flowers and fruit and little speckled eggs, and that funny bird flying around her head. Little bits of eggshell were falling down the back of Mama's neck.

"AND THE ANGEL SAID, BE NOT AFRAID!" Preacher Jurkins shouted again.

"Uhhh, Mama," I said.

"Shhh . . . ," Mama said. She was full into the sermon.

I turned to my other side. "Uhhh, Daddy," I said.

"Shhh, Tandy."

**"AND PEOPLE BELIEVED OR
THEY DIDN'T BELIEVE!"**

By then enough people around us noticed that Mama's hat was acting up, and they started nudging each other. The eggs were hatching right off Mama's hat! Even Preacher Jurkins stopped his sermonizing.

Mama finally felt something peculiar going on, and she tried to bat the bird away from her like a pesky fly.

The preacher pointed to her from the pulpit. A big wide finger. "Sister Fannie Mae. Don't move! A miracle is taking place!"

By now the baby birds were tapping their heads against their shells, and the mother bird had landed on top of the hat and was helping them with the rest of the job.

"IT'S A MIRACLE!" said the preacher.

"A miracle," repeated Daddy.

"Miracle, miracle, miracle!" the rest of the church echoed.

Then the mother bird settled down atop Mama's hat and started tending to her babies. There was much Hallelujah and Praise the Lord after that. The choir sang and the birds sang and Mama looked proud because she was part of this miracle.

Doves fly all through the Old Testament, but this was the first starling that made an appearance in church. Mama said it reminded her kind of like the true meaning of Easter, because it's a time for believing in miracles. New life is such a pretty little thing, and now here were four tiny birds, their eyes still closed, trusting their mama would take care of them no matter what.

Mama carried the hat home carefully, the mother bird flying alongside of her, and all the ladies from our church, trooping behind like they were on their way to Galilee.

When we got home, Mama made Daddy get the ladder and put it against the tallest apple tree. Then Mama climbed all the way up herself—my mama could do anything—and placed the hat with the family of birds in it snugly against the branches, where the sun could warm their backs and no cat could catch them.

At first I was a little disappointed that we weren't going to see her wearing that fine new Easter hat anymore. But then I thought about how the hat would keep those baby birds safe and protected the rest of the spring till they were ready to fly out on their own. "Mama," I said, "you made a very good choice indeed." Daddy winked at me.

We never figured out exactly how real bird eggs wound up in Mama's fine new Easter hat. As Mama said, miracles aren't ours to figure out.

Mama's hat stayed there a long time. We had beautiful music the rest of that spring. The next spring, another family hatched there. And the spring after that, the starlings and finches and thrushes and red-tailed warblers took what was left of the decorations. The other birds pulled threads out one at a time and flew off to make their nests until you couldn't see anything in the tree anymore that even looked like it could have been part of a hat. Except maybe you could imagine long, wispy threads floating in and out of the highest branches and winding around the apple blossoms.

But all that summer in between, when you could still see the hat up there, Daddy and me would go out on the front porch swing late in the day. Sometimes folks would pass by on the street and wave, and they'd point up into the apple tree.

"Fine hat, Hayman!" they said.

"None finer," replied Daddy.

And that was true.